P9-DVD-161

CH

DEC 09

Westminster Public Library
3705 W. 112th Ave.
Westminster, CO 80031
www.westminsterlibrary.org

A Note to Parents and Caregivers:

Read-it! Readers are for children who are just starting on the amazing road to reading. These beautiful books support both the acquisition of reading skills and the love of books.

 The PURPLE LEVEL presents basic topics and objects using high frequency words and simple language patterns.

 The RED LEVEL presents familiar topics using common words and repeating sentence patterns.

 The BLUE LEVEL presents new ideas using a larger vocabulary and varied sentence structure.

 The YELLOW LEVEL presents more challenging ideas, a broad vocabulary, and wide variety in sentence structure.

 The GREEN LEVEL presents more complex ideas, an extended vocabulary range, and expanded language structures.

 The ORANGE LEVEL presents a wide range of ideas and concepts using challenging vocabulary and complex language structures.

When sharing a book with your child, read in short stretches, pausing often to talk about the pictures. Have your child turn the pages and point to the pictures and familiar words. And be sure to reread favorite stories or parts of stories.

There is no right or wrong way to share books with children. Find time to read with your child, and pass on the legacy of literacy.

Adria F. Klein, Ph.D.
Professor Emeritus
California State University
San Bernardino, California

Editor: Christianne Jones
Designer: Lori Bye
Page Production: Michelle Biedscheid
Art Director: Nathan Gassman
The illustrations in this book were created with watercolor and pencil.

Picture Window Books
151 Good Counsel Drive
P.O. Box 669
Mankato, MN 56002-0669
877-845-8392
www.picturewindowbooks.com

Copyright © 2009 by Picture Window Books
All rights reserved. No part of this book may be reproduced without written
permission from the publisher. The publisher takes no responsibility for the use of
any of the materials or methods described in this book, nor for the products thereof.

Printed in the United States of America.

All books published by Picture Window Books
are manufactured with paper containing at least
10 percent post-consumer waste.

Library of Congress Cataloging-in-Publication Data
Worsham, Adria F. (Adria Fay), 1947-
Max celebrates Ramadan / by Adria F. Worsham ; illustrated by
Mernie Gallagher-Cole.
p. cm. — (Read-it! readers: the life of Max)
ISBN 978-1-4048-4762-0 (library binding)
[1. Ramadan—Fiction. 2. Muslims—Fiction.] I. Gallagher-Cole, Mernie, ill.
II. Title.
PZ7.W887835May 2008
[E]—dc22   2008006315

Max
Celebrates
Ramadan

by Adria F. Worsham
illustrated by Mernie Gallagher-Cole

Special thanks to our advisers:

Mohammed Abdul Aleem, CEO and Editor
The Global Muslim eCommunity: IslamiCity.com

Susan Kesselring, M.A., Literacy Educator
Rosemount–Apple Valley–Eagan (Minnesota) School District

PiCTURE WiNDOW BOOKS
Minneapolis, Minnesota

Max and Omar are good friends.
Max is going to Omar's house.

Omar's family is Muslim. They believe in the religion called Islam.

Omar's family is having a big feast to celebrate the end of Ramadan.

Omar tells Max that adults and some older children fast during Ramadan. They do not eat or drink anything during the day.

He tells Max that Ramadan lasts for one month.

During Ramadan, Muslim people read their holy book. It is called the *Quran*.

Omar's whole family is at the house. His aunts, uncles, and cousins are there, too.

They are all there for this joyful day.

Everyone has brought special foods to share.

Omar tells Max that fasting teaches people to give.

Max and Omar help set the table.

Looking at all the good food makes them hungry. They can't wait to eat!

Omar's father tells Max that this special holiday is called Eid-al-Fitr.

17

Eid-al-Fitr means "Celebration of the end of fasting." It marks the end of the month of Ramadan.

Omar's family is happy that Max joined them for the celebration.

Max thanks Omar and his family.

Max learned a lot about Ramadan.

More *Read-it!* Readers

Bright pictures and fun stories help you practice your reading skills. Look for more books at your level.

Max Goes on the Bus
Max Goes Shopping
Max Goes to School
Max Goes to the Barber
Max Goes to the Dentist
Max Goes to the Doctor
Max Goes to the Library
Max Goes to the Playground

Max and Buddy Go to the Vet
Max and the Adoption Day Party
Max Celebrates Chinese New Year
Max Celebrates Cinco de Mayo
Max Celebrates Groundhog Day
Max Celebrates Martin Luther
  King Jr. Day
Max Goes to a Cookout
Max Goes to the Farm
Max Goes to the Grocery Store
Max Learns Sign Language
Max Stays Overnight
Max's Fun Day

On the Web

FactHound offers a safe, fun way to find Web sites related to topics in this book. All of the sites on FactHound have been researched by our staff.

1. Visit *www.facthound.com*

2. Type in this special code: 1404847626

3. Click on the FETCH IT button.

Your trusty FactHound will fetch the best sites for you!
A complete list of *Read-it!* Readers is available on our Web site:
www.picturewindowbooks.com

24